by John Sazaklis

THE HOPPING HERO

illustrated by Art Baltazar

Picture Window Books™
a capstone imprint

Starring...

HOPPY
THE MARVEL BUNNY!

SOBEK!

MR. MIND!

TAWKY TAWNY!

TABLE OF CONTENTS!

SUPER-PET HERO FILE 007:
HOPPY

Ultra-hearing

Wisdom

Flight

Super-strength

Courage

Super-speed

Super Hero Owner:
CAPTAIN MARVEL

Species: Bunny

Place of Birth: Animalville

Age: Unknown

Favorite Food: Carrots

Bio: One day, Hoppy spoke the magic word "Shazam!" and gained the same superpowers as his hero, Captain Marvel.

Super-Pet Enemy File 007:
SOBEK

Razor-sharp Teeth —

Super-strength —

Razor-sharp Claws —

Super-villain Owner:
BLACK ADAM

Super-Pet Enemy File 007B:
MR. MIND

Super Intelligence —
Mind Control —
Voice Transmitter —

Super-villain Partner:
DR. SIVANA

Chapter 1

SHAZAM!

On a sunny day, **Hoppy** the bunny met two of his friends at the Fawcett City Animal Festival.

Millie the rabbit wanted to enjoy the rides, attractions, and games. **Tawky Tawny** the tiger looked forward to all the food!

"Thanks for spending the day with me," Hoppy said to his friends. "It's nice to relax and have a little fun."

"Ooh, look!" Millie pointed to a nearby game. "Let's see if Hoppy is as strong as Marvel Bunny!"

Unlike Tawky Tawny, Millie didn't know that Hoppy *was* **Marvel Bunny.** Each time Hoppy said the word **"SHAZAM!,"** a bolt of lightning gave him the power of six species. These powers had to be kept secret.

THE WISDOM OF SALAMANDER!

THE POWER OF ZEBREUS!

THE STRENGTH OF HOGULES!

THE COURAGE OF ABALONE!

THE STAMINA OF ANTLERS!

THE SPEED OF MONKURY!

Millie pulled Hoppy over to the game. It was called Test Your Might.

Players used a rubber hammer to whack a metal target. A scale measured each person's strength.

Hoppy blushed. "I don't think that's such a good idea —" he began.

Suddenly, the friends heard screams on the other side of the festival.

The carousel was spinning out of control and falling apart! The colorful horses were flying in all directions.

Little animals clung to the ride. They cried out in fear. Their parents stood frozen in shock. No one could get near the machine without getting hurt.

"Mmm!" said Tawky Tawny, rubbing his tummy. "I sure am hungry!"

"How can you think of food at a time like this?!" Millie shouted.

"I'll get some hot dogs!" Hoppy said, running into the empty snack tent.

"Hot dogs?! But lives are in danger!" cried Millie. **"Who will help us?"**

In the distance, Tawky Tawny heard
the rumble of thunder and the crash of
lightning. "Oh, I have a good feeling
help is on the way," the tiger replied
with a smile.

"SHAZAM!"

In a flash, **Hoppy changed into Marvel Bunny.** He rushed to the rescue.

At the same time, the carousel spun faster and faster. Tawky Tawny darted on all fours into the path of danger. He tried to control the crowd.

"Everybody back!" the tiger yelled, pushing onlookers with his paws.

Suddenly, one of the carousel horses flew toward the crowd. A blur of yellow and pink zoomed by overhead.

WOOOOSH!

Marvel Bunny reined in the plastic stallion. He placed it safely on the ground. Then he saved two baby otters and returned them to their parents.

Suddenly, more parts of the ride broke off. More screams were heard.

A piece of wood had trapped Mr. and Mrs. Sloth. Tawky Tawny heard their cries and went to help! The tiger lifted the debris off the animals, placed them on his back, and ran to safety.

Tawky Tawny ran faster and faster as the rubble got closer and closer.

Meanwhile, Marvel Bunny sped toward the carousel's controls. The power switch had been broken off. He couldn't shut off the machine!

Using his gift of wisdom, Marvel Bunny reached under the controls. He started taking apart the engine. His paws moved at super-speed. Soon, a flurry of gears and bolts littered the ground around him.

SKREEEECH!!

The crumbling machine finally slowed to a stop. Marvel Bunny zipped around. He brought each crying child back to his or her parents.

Then Marvel Bunny landed next to Tawky Tawny. **"Phew!"** the hero sighed. **"I'm glad that's over."**

Tawky Tawny leaned against a plastic horse that had escaped the carousel. "Indeed," he replied. "Too much horseplay for my taste!"

"Someone must have messed with the controls," Marvel Bunny said.

Millie hopped over. "Oh, gosh!" she said, blushing. "Marvel Bunny! Here! I must thank you!"

Millie closed her eyes and puckered her lips. She leaned in for a kiss.

"Um, if you'll excuse me," the hero said, turning redder than his uniform. "I have a job to finish."

He flew into the sky as Millie fell forward and **smooched the horse!**

Moments later, Hoppy returned with the hot dogs. As he walked toward his friends, something caught his eye.

A crocodile tail disappeared behind a tent. When Hoppy turned the corner, the tail and its owner were gone!

"This can't be!" the bunny said.

Just then, Hoppy's friends spotted him. Millie was very excited. She couldn't stop talking about Marvel Bunny. Tawky Tawny took his hot dog from Hoppy. He swallowed it in one gulp and passed Millie hers.

"Thanks, but no thanks," she said. "I am too excited to eat. Did you see Marvel Bunny? **He's so dreamy!"**

Tawky Tawny helped himself to Millie's hot dog as well.

Then Tawky Tawny put his paw on Hoppy's shoulder. "What's the matter, dear friend?" he asked.

"I can't eat either," Hoppy said. "I think I saw Sobek."

Tawky Tawny swallowed hard. "That can't be," the tiger said with surprise. "Sobek the Croc is just a myth, right? No one's actually seen him before!"

Hoppy shook his head. **"He's real,"** he replied. **"And he's up to no good."**

Chapter 2

REPTILE RAIDER

Everyone in Fawcett City had heard stories of **Sobek**. The croc's big sharp teeth often gave children nightmares.

In real life, however, Sobek was simply an oversized scaredy-croc. He was embarrassed by his crooked teeth and ran from his own shadow.

On most days, Sobek hid in the deep, dark sewers. In fact, he didn't know why he had come to the Animal Festival or broken the carousel today.

When he realized what he had done, Sobek ran away in tears.

Then, suddenly, a tiny voice echoed in his head. "Stop sniveling, you weakling!" the voice commanded. "Your mind is under my control."

Sobek stared blankly into the distance. **"Yes, master,"** he replied.

"Go back to that festival and cause more trouble. It's the only way to lure Marvel Bunny into my trap," the voice continued. "Once you are both in my control, I will create the Monster Society of Evil!"

Back at the festival, everything had returned to normal. But Hoppy was still on edge. He had a feeling that more trouble was on the way.

"Let's get some ice cream to calm our nerves," Tawky Tawny said.

Millie agreed. Together, they walked over to Mr. Seal, the ice cream seller.

Without warning, more screams and gasps came from the crowd. Tawky Tawny's hair stood on end. He looked at the fairgrounds and saw . . . **Sobek!**

"Can it be?" someone cried.

"He's real, and I knew it,"
Hoppy said, gritting his teeth.

Sobek climbed onto the Ferris wheel.
He waited for the next seat to come his
way. Then he ripped it off the hinges!

The reptile raider snarled and lifted the chair high above his head. With a roar, he hurled it toward the innocent animals below.

"Oh no, not again!" Millie cried. She looked over at Hoppy. The bunny was nowhere to be seen.

Hoppy quickly hopped behind the festival's dunk tank and looked around. The coast was clear.

A bolt of lighting changed Hoppy into Marvel Bunny. The hero zoomed toward the Ferris wheel. He caught the falling seat.

In the meantime, Tawky Tawny shook off his coat and glasses. He raced toward the attraction. Marvel Bunny needed his help!

The tiger climbed the Ferris wheel and sneaked behind Sobek. The croc was busy destroying the ride.

"Relax," Tawky Tawny yelled at Sobek. "And have a seat!"

THWAAACK!

The tiger tackled the crocodile. They tumbled into the another seat on the Ferris wheel.

Using his front paws, Tawky Tawny pinned Sobek down on his back. During the struggle, the tiger discovered a small worm sitting atop Sobek's head.

Tawky Tawny blinked with surprise.

It was **Mr. Mind**, Marvel Bunny's enemy! The wicked worm had mind controlling powers. And, despite his size, he had grand plans.

Suddenly, the day's events all made sense. Mr. Mind had been controlling Sobek. The crocodile wasn't able to stop himself.

"It ends here, Mr. Mind!" yelled Tawky Tawny, reaching for the worm.

Mr. Mind shot a super-strong web, trapping the tiger in a silky bond.

"Throw this troublesome tiger overboard!" Mr. Mind yelled to Sobek.

The croc obeyed. He lifted Tawky Tawny over his head.

Ugh! I shouldn't have eaten all those hot dogs, thought Talky Tawny.

Suddenly, the tiger was falling through the air. The ground was rushing up at him.

Tawky Tawny shut his eyes. Certain doom was down below, and those hot dogs were coming back up.

Chapter 3

WICKED WORM

"Need a lift?"

Tawky Tawny heard a voice and opened his eyes. He hovered in midair.

His best friend in the world flew up to save him! Marvel Bunny carried the tiger to an empty Ferris wheel seat.

"Sit tight," said Marvel Bunny. "I

must stop Sobek before it's too late."

Sobek growled and grabbed Marvel

Bunny in a bear hug.

Down below, Millie was watching with worry. She ran to a kind bird named Doctor Falcon. "You have to get me up there," she pleaded. **"They need our help!"**

Doctor Falcon agreed. He picked Millie up. Together, they flew toward Tawky Tawny. **WHOOSH!**

Using teeth and talons, they ripped through his silky bonds.

"Thank you, sir," said the tiger, turning to join the fight.

Meanwhile, Marvel Bunny finally broke free from Sobek's grasp. The enemies fell off the Ferris wheel.

SPLASH!

They both landed in the dunk tank. The shock broke Sobek out of Mr. Mind's spell.

Marvel Bunny caught the wicked worm before he could inch away. "I'm not surprised that you're behind this," said the hero.

"You'll change your tune once you see things my way," Mr. Mind replied. The villain quickly put Marvel Bunny into a trance.

"Yes, master," the hero replied.

"Together, we will rule the animals of Fawcett City," added Marvel Bunny. "All hail the Monster Society of Evil!"

"Great minds think alike!" said Mr. Mind, twitching with evil glee.

"What have you done to my hero!" Millie shouted at Mr. Mind.

Her cries broke the villain's focus and his evil spell! Summoning all his powers, Marvel Bunny flew Mr. Mind away from the festival.

When they were alone, Marvel Bunny opened his fist and looked at his enemy. "It's time to put an end to your mind games," the hero yelled.

A bolt of lightning ripped through the sky. It blasted them both.

Marvel Bunny was now good old Hoppy. Mr. Mind had passed out. A plume of smoke lifted off the worm's antennae. Mr. Mind wouldn't remember a thing when he woke up.

In the meantime, Tawky Tawny called the police. When Hoppy returned to the festival, he turned over the worm to the officers.

"Marvel Bunny had to run," said Hoppy, "but he gave me this instruction: 'Lock up Mr. Mind where he will have no visitors.' **It is the only way to make his powers useless.**"

The police were very careful. They placed the worm inside a lead box with breathing holes. Then they drove off to Fawcett City Jail.

Millie ran over to Hoppy. "Wow!"

she said. "You're so brave! Come on,

I'll buy you some ice cream."

"What about my new friend?" asked

Hoppy, pointing toward Sobek.

"The more, the merrier!" said Millie.

Everyone at the festival cheered.

Sure, some of the rides had been damaged, but the day was saved. Seeing Marvel Bunny in action was more exciting than all the amusement parks in Fawcett City combined!

KNOW YOUR HERO PETS!

1. Krypto
2. Streaky
3. Beppo
4. Comet
5. Ace
6. Robin Robin
7. Jumpa
8. Whatzit
9. Storm
10. Topo
11. Ark
12. Hoppy
13. Batcow
14. Big Ted
15. Proty
16. Gleek
17. Paw Pooch
18. Bull Dog
19. Chameleon Collie
20. Hot Dog
21. Tail Terrier
22. Tusky Husky
23. Mammoth Mutt
24. Dawg
25. B'dg
26. Stripezoid
27. Zallion
28. Ribitz
29. Bzzd
30. Gratch
31. Buzzoo
32. Fossfur
33. Zhoomp
34. Eeny

AW YEAH, JOKES!

What kind of books do bunnies read?

No idea.

The ones with hoppy endings!

Why did the bunnies go on strike?

Why?

They wanted a raise in celery!

Why did the bunny go to the barber?

No clue.

He needed a hare cut.

WORD POWER!

carousel (KER-uh-sell)—an revolving amusement park ride, also known as a merry-go-round

debris (duh-BREE)—the scattered pieces of something that has been broken

society (suh-SYE-uh-tee)—a group for people who share the same interests

species (SPEE-sheez)—one of the groups into which animals are divided based on common traits

stallion (STAL-yuhn)—an adult male horse

trance (TRANSS)—a feeling of being sleepy and under the control of another

wisdom (WIZ-duhm)—knowledge, experience, and good judgement

MEET THE AUTHOR!

John Sazaklis

John Sazaklis spent part of life working in a family coffee shop, the House of Donuts. The other part, he spent drawing and writing stories. He has illustrated Spider-Man books and written Batman books for HarperCollins. John lives in the Big Apple and takes a bite out of it every day.

MEET THE ILLUSTRATOR!

Eisner Award-winner Art Baltazar

Art Baltazar is a cartoonist machine from the heart of Chicago! He defines cartoons and comics not only as an art style, but as a way of life. Currently, Art is the creative force behind *The New York Times* best-selling, Eisner Award-winning, DC Comics series Tiny Titans, and the co-writer for *Billy Batson and the Magic of SHAZAM!* Art is living the dream! He draws comics and never has to leave the house. He lives with his lovely wife, Rose, big boy Sonny, little boy Gordon, and little girl Audrey. Right on!

ART BALTAZAR says:

Read all of the DC SUPER-PETS stories today!

▦ Picture Window Books™

Published in 2012
A Capstone Imprint
151 Good Counsel Drive, P.O. Box 669
Mankato, Minnesota 56002
www.capstonepub.com

Cataloging-in-Publication Data is available
at the Library of Congress website.
ISBN: 978-1-4048-6477-1 (library binding)
ISBN: 978-1-4048-6843-4 (paperback)

Summary: Sobek the evil crocodile is on the
loose! Luckily, Hoppy is close by. With the
powers of six species, this heroic hare will
wipe the smile from Sobek's face and bounce
the reptile raider back to the bayou.

Art Director & Designer: Bob Lentz
Editor: Donald Lemke
Creative Director: Heather Kindseth
Editorial Director: Michael Dahl

Printed in the United States of America
in Stevens Point, Wisconsin.
082011   006341R